OTIS THE OWL

BY MARY HOLLAND

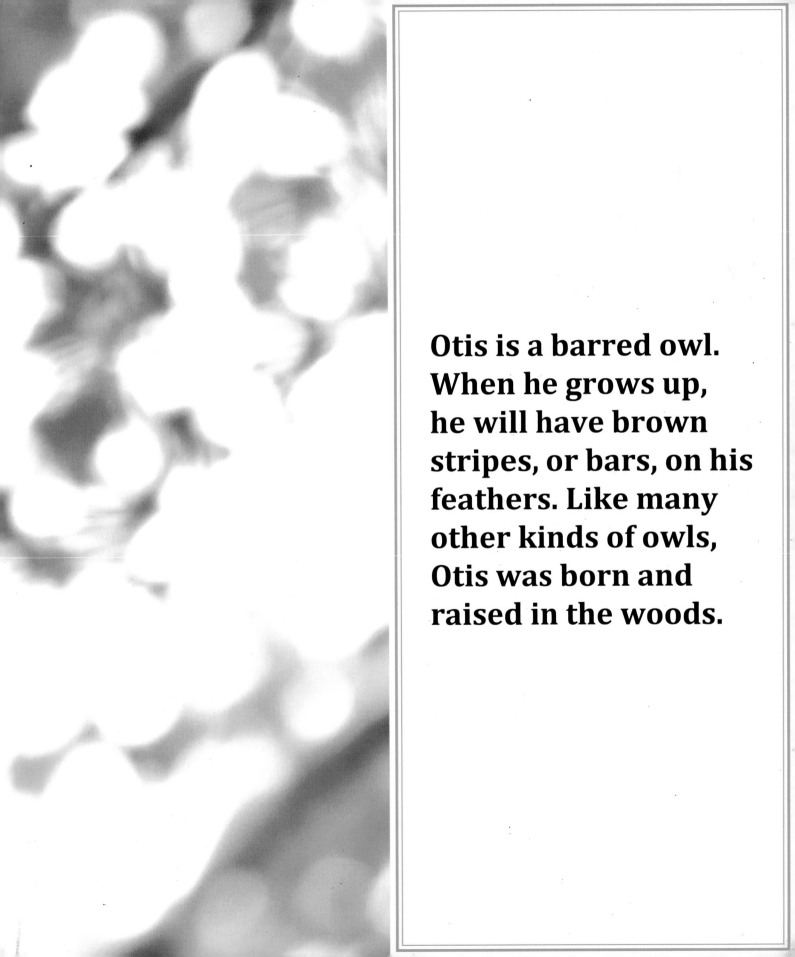

Otis is a barred owl. When he grows up, he will have brown stripes, or bars, on his feathers. Like many other kinds of owls, Otis was born and raised in the woods.

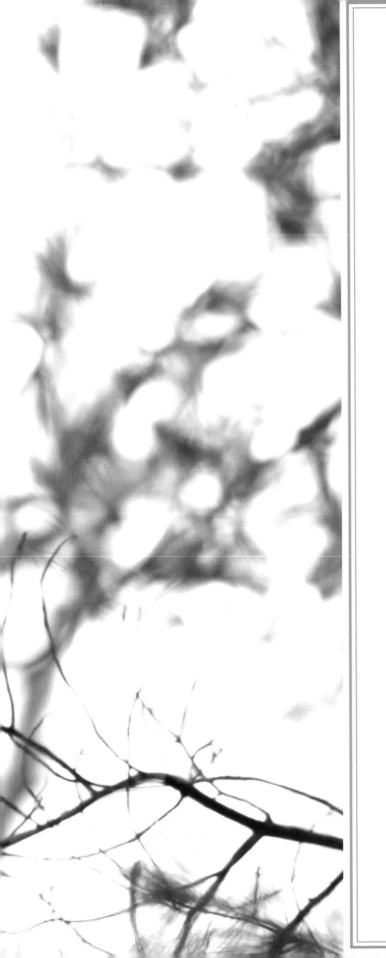

One day when there was still snow on the ground, Otis' mother and father found a hole, or cavity, in a tree. They decided it would make a perfect nest for their chicks. It had a roof over it that would keep the snow and rain out.

The mother owl laid her eggs at the bottom of the tree cavity. She sat on the eggs to keep them warm. Four weeks later, in the spring when most of the snow had melted, the eggs hatched and out came Otis.

After living for a month or so in the deep, dark cavity, Otis climbs up to the opening, using his talons and beak to cling to the inside of the tree. With his large eyes, Otis looks at the outside world for the first time.

Otis still has some of the white, fuzzy down feathers he was born with, but new feathers are growing in underneath them.

All of a sudden, another owl chick appears—Otis has a sister!

Otis' mother and father are predators. They eat other animals (prey). They use their powerful feet and sharp claws (talons) to catch and kill their prey.

When Otis grows up, he will eat most of his prey whole, but while he is young, his parents use their strong, curved beaks to tear his food into small pieces that Otis can swallow.

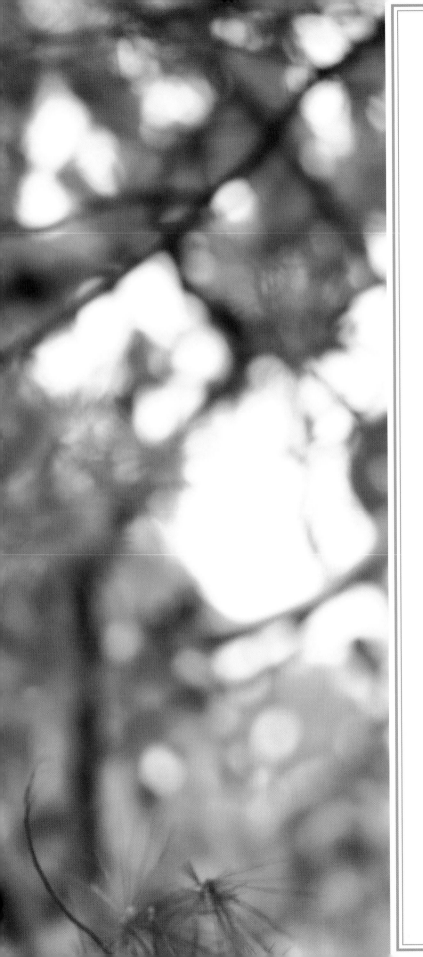

Otis' parents are busy catching and bringing prey to the nest for the young owls to eat. Otis' favorite meals are mice, chipmunks and voles.

Usually owls are active at night (nocturnal) and sleep during the day. But when they are raising their babies, owls hunt both day and night.

As Otis and his sister grow bigger, they are able to swallow most of their meals whole.

Can you find the vole that Otis' father just brought him?

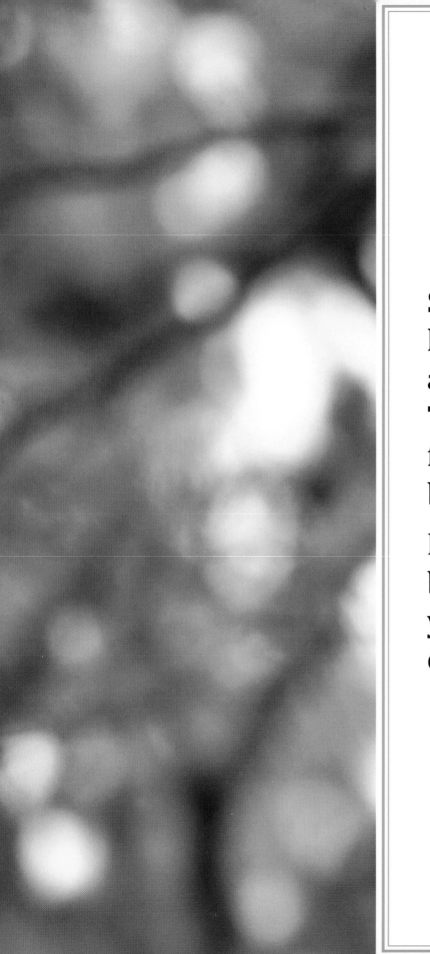

Sometimes Otis and his sister don't get along very well. They fight over the food their parents bring them.

Do you have a brother or sister you argue with once in a while?

At other times, Otis and his sister are best friends. They even comb (preen) each other's feathers with their beaks.

Otis and his sister take turns watching for their mother and father to return home with food. It is Otis' turn to stand watch at the nest hole.

Can you find Otis' sister's beak?

While waiting for his next meal to be delivered, Otis practices flapping his wings. He will need strong muscles in order to fly.

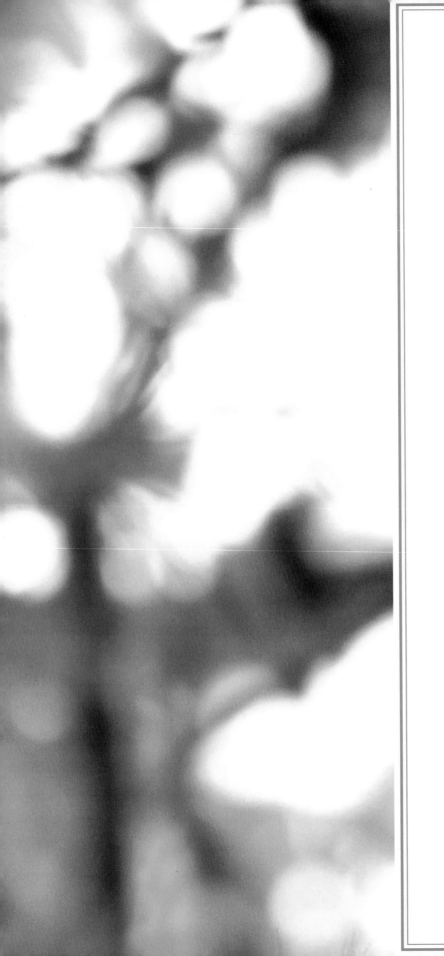

Finally, Otis is ready to leave his nest and explore the world. He looks down at the ground, which seems very far away. Otis has to be brave if he is going to leave home, as he can't fly yet.

What do you think he decides to do?

Otis finds the courage to climb out and perch on a nearby limb. Soon his sister follows him.

Otis' parents continue to bring them food. In about a month, Otis will be able to fly short distances. By the end of the summer, he will be catching his own meals.

For Creative Minds

Owl Pellets

When an owl eats a mouse or other prey, there are parts (nails, teeth, bones, skulls, fur, feathers) that are hard to digest. These parts are packed together into a pellet inside the owl. An owl coughs up about two pellets a day, roughly six to twelve hours after it eats. Because an owl usually swallows its prey whole, a pellet often contains the prey's whole skeleton. The bones and teeth are wrapped in fur. This fur protects the owl's throat when the owl coughs up the pellet.

Many birds cough up pellets, not just owls. Usually, the larger the bird, the larger the pellet. Barred owls weigh 1.6 pounds. Barred owl pellets are about two inches long. Snowy owls weigh 4 pounds. Snowy owl pellets are about five inches long.

snowy owl pellet

barred owl pellet

If you find where an owl has roosted, you may discover one or more pellets on the ground beneath the roost. If you take a pellet apart, you can often tell exactly what kind of prey the owl ate from the bones and skulls that are in it.

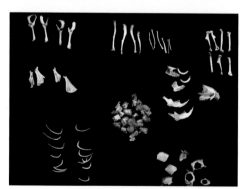

barred owl pellet (dissected)

Which of These Does an Owl Eat?

Which of these animals do you think owls can eat? Answers are below.

eastern chipmunk

green frog

meadow vole

ruffed grouse

common garter snake

red squirrel

striped skunk

woodchuck

Answer: All of them

Owl Anatomy

Owls, eagles, hawks, falcons, and ospreys are raptors, or birds of prey. Raptors feed on other animals (prey), including mice, voles, rabbits, opossums, frogs, snakes and even skunks. Most raptors have excellent eyesight, strong beaks, and sharp talons (claws). These help them hunt, catch, kill, and eat their prey.

Match the photo to the description of the body part on the next page.

northern hawk owl

A — great horned owl

B — barred owl

C — barn owl

D — snowy owl

E — great gray owl

F — barred owl

Eyes. Most owls are active at night. Their eyes are large in order to collect light so that they can see where to fly and find prey to eat. The eyes of most birds are on the sides of their face, but owl eyes are in the front. This helps owls tell how far away a mouse or squirrel is. Owls cannot move their eyes to the left or right; they can only see straight ahead. In order to see to either side, owls must turn their entire head. Because owls have 14 neck bones (twice as many as humans), they can turn their head three-quarters of the way around in either direction in order to see behind them.

Owls can see well at night, but they can also see in the day.

Facial Disc. Each owl eye is located in the middle of a round circle of feathers called a facial disc. These special feathers collect sound and help owls hear soft noises by directing sound waves to their ears. Owls that hunt only at night tend to have large facial discs, as they have to listen for prey in the dark.

Have a friend say something softly to you from across the room. Then cup your hands behind your ears and have your friend repeat what he or she said. Can you hear better with or without your "discs" or hands?

Talons. The claws on an owl's toes are called talons. They are long, curved, and very sharp. Birds of prey use their feet and talons to catch and kill their prey. Bigger owls usually have bigger talons and can catch larger prey.

Three toes on each foot point forward and one toe points backwards. If their prey is struggling, owls can rotate one of their front toes to the back, in order to get a better grip on their prey.

Beak. An owl's beak is short and curved downward. It helps them hold prey and tear it for their young. If it stuck straight out, an owl's beak might make it hard for the owl to see. Owls normally eat their prey whole, but if their prey is too big to swallow, they use their beak to tear it into small pieces.

Feathers. Owls fly and glide silently. Their feathers are velvety thick and soft, absorbing a lot of the sound of their flight. Unlike other raptors, they also have a comb-like fringe on the outer edge of their first few wing feathers that muffles sound and helps them fly quietly. Owls can hear their prey, but their prey has a hard time hearing them.

Why would an owl not want to make any sound when it is flying?

Ears. An owl's ears are on the sides of its head, not the top. The feathers that stick up on some owls are tufts of feathers, not ears. It is hard to see an owl's ears, as they are usually covered with facial disc feathers. Owl ears are simply holes in the sides of the owl's head. If an owl's ears stuck out from its head like a human's ears do, they would not be able to fly as well as they do.

Answers: A-beak. B-ears. C-facial disc. D-eyes. E-feathers. F-talons.

To Otis Sumner Brown, may you never lose your sense of wonder for the natural world—MH

Many thanks to the Vermont Institute of Natural Science, which provided photographic subjects for many of the owls pictured in *For Creative Minds*. (Otis is a wild bird, photographed in the wild.)

Thanks to Margaret Fowle, Conservation Biologist with Audubon Vermont, and to Sandy Beck, Education Director of the St. Francis Wildlife Association, for verifying the accuracy of the information in this book.

Library of Congress Cataloging-in-Publication Data

Names: Holland, Mary, 1946- author.
Title: Otis the owl / by Mary Holland.
Description: Mount Pleasant, SC : Arbordale Publishing, [2017] | Audience: Ages 4-8. | Audience: K to grade 3. | Includes bibliographical references.
Identifiers: LCCN 2016043593 (print) | LCCN 2016045559 (ebook) | ISBN 9781628559392 (english hardcover) | ISBN 9781628559408 (english pbk.) | ISBN 9781628559415 (spanish pbk.) | ISBN 9781628559422 (English

Downloadable eBook) | ISBN 9781628559446 (English Interactive Dual-Language eBook) | ISBN 9781628559439 (Spanish Downloadable eBook) | ISBN 9781628559453 (Spanish Interactive Dual-Language eBook)
Subjects: LCSH: Barred owl--Infancy--Juvenile literature. | Owls--Juvenile literature.
Classification: LCC QL696.S83 H65 2017 (print) | LCC QL696.S83 (ebook) | DDC 598.9/7--dc23
LC record available at https://lccn.loc.gov/2016043593

Translated into Spanish: *Otis, el búho*

Lexile® Level: 870L

key phrases: birds of prey, barred owl, food, growth and change, learned behavior, life cycle, owl, physical adaptation, raptors

Otis Sumner Brown

Bibliography:
"Barred Owl." All About Birds. Cornell Lab of Ornithology, n.d. Web. 13 Sept. 2016.
"Barred Owl." Audubon. N.p., 2016. Web. 13 Sept. 2016.
Duncan, James R. *The Complete Book of North American Owls.* San Diego: Thunder Bay, 2013. Print.
Lewis, Deane. "Information about Owls." The Owl Pages. N.p., n.d. Web. 13 Sept. 2016.
Rogers, Denny, and Lori Corbett. *The Illustrated Owl: Barn, Barred, & Great Horned.* East Petersburg, PA: Fox Chapel Pub., 2008. Print.
Weidensaul, Scott. *Owls of North America and the Caribbean.* Boston: Houghton Mifflin Harcourt, 2015. Print.

Manufactured in China, December 2016
This product conforms to CPSIA 2008
First Printing

Arbordale Publishing
Mt. Pleasant, SC 29464
www.ArbordalePublishing.com